# About Gary

The Author

Gary is a boogie bug who lives with his wife Stacey and their 2 little buglets, Jam-Sandwich and Molly Pops. He loves daydreaming about toys when he is not writing stories about the folk of Yummy Mead. His most favourite things are drinking pop and napping in the sun!

# About Debra

## The Illustrator

Debra is a doodle bug who fills her days with painting, drawing and sitting in her squiggly tree capturing Yummy Mead's antics in her sketchbook. She loves listening to the rain, eating cake and creating wonderful worlds.

For Am-Jams and Molly-Pops
GP

For Carol and Barry
DH

First Published 2015 by Jam-Sandwich Publishing
67 Christchurch Road, Hemel Hempstead
Hertfordshire, HP2 5BY

First paperback edition printed 2015

Printed in China

For more copies of this book, please email: hello@Jam-Sandwich.co.uk

Copy Set by Robert J Pritchard.

A catalogue record for this book is available from the British Library.

ISBN 978-0-9932746-0-2

In the land of Yummy Mead,

there stood a wood
of magic leaves.

Nestled in the golden tree,

sat Amber-Jam the honey bee.

Thoughtful, clever,
trustworthy...

...keeper of the
treasure key.

Yummy's insects did agree
that Amber was just...

...Heavenly!

But Greedy Spider could not see
Jam's kindness, through her Golden Tree!

With googly eyes and knobbly knees...

Spider's breath would make you

# Wheeze!

Yummy's insects did decree
that Spider was unsavoury!

With arms wrapped 'round her Golden Key
Amber perched so daintily.

Chilling in the Ice Cream Tree,

was Willy Woo, the Worker Bee.

Yummy's insects did agree

that Willy was...

...Exemplary!

One afternoon, a tick past three,

Willy poured himself some

TEA.

"I wish I had a friend with me,
        to share my cake and watch TV".

Then dancing in the doughnut tree...

Willy sensed a far off plea.

HELPPPP!

HELP ME!

Way up high there wept a bee,

AHHHHHH!

HELP MEEEEEE!!!

AHHHHHH!!

AHHHHH!

trapped in branches

of her TREE.

Spider, spider,
please,
please,
PLEASE

...do not steal my precious leaves.

Sneaky spider LOOK AT ME,

I am WOO the WORKER BEE!

"Spider, what a shameful deed!
They're not your leaves
you're full of
greed!

You deserve the ponky tree,

its more your style, I guarantee!"

Willy buzzed 'round gaining speed

and with a whizz his Love was freed.

Hand in hand they made a breeze,

buzzing through the magic...

...LEAVES

"Willy, you're the kindest Bee,
let's fly together, YOU and ME".

"Firstly, will you MARRY ME?"

Asked Willy,
smiling bashfully.

"I DO"

Before the spring the happy bees...